This book belongs to

....

Copyright © 2016

make believe ideas ltd

The Wilderness, Berkhamsted, Hertfordshire, HP4 2AZ, UK.
501 Nelson Place, P.O. Box 141000, Nashville, TN 37214-1000, USA.

www.makebelieveideas.com

Original poem by Clement Clarke Moore.
Illustrated by Clare Fennell.

'Twas the Night Before Christmas

Clement Clarke Moore

•

Clare Fennell

make
believe
ideas

'Twas the night before Christmas, when all through the house
not a creature was stirring, not even a mouse.
The stockings were hung by the chimney with care,
in hopes that St. Nicholas soon would be there.

The children were nestled all **snug** in their beds,
while visions of *sugarplums* danced in their heads.

And *Mama* in her 'kerchief, and I in my cap,
had just settled our brains for a long *winter's* nap.

When out on the lawn there arose such a clatter,
I sprang from the bed to see what was the matter.
Away to the window

I flew like a flash,
tore open
the shutters and
threw up
the sash.

The moon, on the breast of the new-fallen snow, gave the luster of mid-day to objects below.

When, what to my wondering
eyes should appear . . .

. . . but a miniature *sleigh* and eight tiny reindeer,

with a little old driver, so *lively* and quick,

I knew in a moment it must be *St. Nick.*

More **rapid** than eagles his **coursers** they came,

and he *whistled,* and **shouted,**

and *called* them by name.

'Now, Dasher! Now, Dancer!

Now, Prancer and Vixen!

On, Comet! On, Cupid!
On, Donner and Blitzen!

To the top of the porch! To the top of the wall!
Now, dash away! Dash away! Dash away all!"

As dry leaves that before the wild hurricane fly,

when they meet with an obstacle, mount to the sky;

so up to the housetop the coursers they flew,

with the sleigh full of toys, and St. Nicholas, too.

And then, in a *twinkling*, I heard on the roof
the **prancing** and *pawing* of each little **hoof**.

As I **drew** in my head, and was turning around,
down the chimney **St. Nicholas** came with a **bound.**

He was **dressed** all in *fur*,
from his **head** to his **foot**,
and his clothes were all **tarnished**
with **ashes** and *soot*.

A **bundle** of *toys*
was **flung** on his back,
and he looked like a **peddler**
just *opening* his pack.

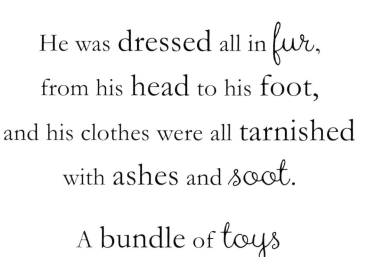

His eyes – how they *twinkled!* His **dimples** – how **merry!**

His **cheeks** were like *roses*, his nose like a **cherry!**

His **droll** little mouth was drawn up like a *bow*,

and the **beard** on his chin was as **white** as the *snow*.

The **stump** of a pipe he held **tight** in his teeth,

and the *smoke*, it encircled his head like a **wreath**.

He had a **broad** face and a little round *belly*
that sh**oo**k when he *laughed*, like a bowlful of jelly!
He was **chubby** and **plump**, a right **jolly** old *elf*,
and I **laughed** when I saw him, in spite of myself.

A **wink** of his eye and a **twist** of his head

soon gave me to know I had **nothing** to dread.

He spoke **not** a word,

but went **straight** to his work,

and **filled** all the *stockings*;

then turned

with a jerk,

and laying his finger

aside of his nose,

and giving a nod,

up the

chimney

he rose!

He sprang to his **sleigh**, to his **team** gave a *whistle*,
and away they all **flew**, like the down of a **thistle**.

But I heard him exclaim, as he drove out of sight,

"Happy Christmas to all,

and to all a good night!"